Ava & Gabby

NINJA
Princess
DETECTIVES

FROGGY
FIASCO

by Kyla Steinkraus

Illustrated by Katie Wood

Rourke
Educational Media
rourkeeducationalmedia.com

A Division of
Carson
Dellosa
Education

www.rourkeeducationalmedia.com

Edited by: Kim Thompson

Cover layout by: Rhea Magaro-Wallace

Interior layout by: Kathy Walsh

Cover and interior illustrations by: Katie Wood

Library of Congress PCN Data

Froggy Fiasco / Kyla Steinkraus
(Ava and Gabby Danger: Ninja Princess Detectives)
ISBN 978-1-73161-485-8 (hard cover) (alk. paper)
ISBN 978-1-73161-292-2 (soft cover)
ISBN 978-1-73161-590-9 (e-Book)
ISBN 978-1-73161-695-1 (ePub)

Library of Congress Control Number: 2019932408

Printed in the United States of America,
North Mankato, Minnesota

Dear Guardian/Educator,
Introduce your child to the wonderful world of reading with our leveled readers. Your growing reader will be continuously engaged as he or she is guided from one level to the next. Each level is carefully built to provide your child with the reading skills and knowledge to be a confident reader! Ultimately, we want your child to develop a love of reading.

Level 1 *Learning to Read*
High frequency words, basic sentences, large type, labels, full color illustrations to help young readers better comprehend the text

Level 2 *Beginning to Read Alone*
Short sentences, familiar words, simple plot, easy-to-read fonts

Level 3 *Reading on Your Own*
Short paragraphs, easy-to-follow plots, vocabulary is increasingly challenging, exciting stories

Level 4 *Proficient Reader*
Chapters, engaging stories, challenging vocabulary, multiple text features

Reading should be a pleasurable experience. A child who enjoys reading reads more, and a child who reads more becomes a better reader. Your child will grow with exposure to broad vocabulary and literary techniques, and will develop deeper critical thinking and comprehension skills. We are excited to be a part of your child's reading journey.

Happy reading,
Rourke Educational Media

Table of Contents

Chapter One

Erk Is Innocent

"Are we finished practicing yet?" Ava Danger asked.

"Pretty please?" her sister, Gabby, asked sweetly.

"We still need to practice your curtsies," Mr. Posh said with a clap of his hands.

Ava and Gabby Danger were all dressed up for the annual Grand Ball later that night. Ava wore her favorite sparkly teal dress. Gabby wore a beautiful purple gown.

They'd been practicing proper manners with Mr. Posh, the palace housekeeper, for what felt like hours.

Gabby curtsied awkwardly. Ava bent her legs and lifted the fluffy ruffles of her dress. Instead of her shiny teal dress shoes, she was still wearing sneakers from their morning Taekwondo class.

"Oops!" Ava said with a sheepish grin.

Mr. Posh pressed the back of his hand to his forehead and sighed. "Whatever will I do with you two? Princesses must know how to curtsy! And with proper shoes!"

Ava and Gabby lived in the palace at the top of the hill with their parents, the king and queen of Klue. While Ava was tall with long straight brown hair, Gabby was short with curly blonde hair springing up all over her head. Ava had glasses, Gabby had none.

They both loved dressing up in fancy dresses. They also loved working up a sweat practicing martial arts. They were ninjas-in-training, after all! They hoped to one day be skilled ninjas like their mother and grandmother. But what Ava and Gabby loved most was a good mystery.

In fact, they were known around Klue as the Ninja Princess Detectives. If anyone in the kingdom had a case to solve, they always came to Ava and Gabby Danger.

Unfortunately, the sisters hadn't come across a good mystery in a whole month. And they'd spent so much time practicing their ninja skills lately, their curtsies had gotten a little rusty.

"Ava, your dress shoes are in the closet, right where I put them," Mr. Posh huffed. He opened the closet door, leaned down, and pushed aside a dozen ruffled, lacy, sequined dresses scattered across the closet floor. Ava was not the neatest princess.

"Ack!" Mr. Posh jumped backward. He pressed his hand over his heart. "What did I tell you about letting Erk hop all over the palace?"

"But he's right here," Ava said.

To prove his innocence, Erk poked his head of out Ava's pocket with a sweet froggy grin.

Erk was their pet frog. Ava and Gabby often wondered if he might be a prince stuck in a frog body. Still, neither wanted to kiss him to find out if it was some kind of magic spell. That was just too gross. Plus, they liked Erk just the way he was.

"Then why is there a frog in the closet?" Mr. Posh cried. "It nearly gave me a heart attack!"

They all stared down at the small, green frog peeking out from a pile of shoes. It looked just like Erk.

"Huh," Gabby grunted.

"How strange," Ava mused.

A frustrated sigh escaped Mr. Posh as he handed Ava her dress shoes. Dark circles shadowed his eyes. "It's my birthday today, you know. I wanted just one day of peace. Just one day!"

Ava felt terrible. "I'm sorry, Mr. Posh. We really do appreciate your help. Everyone in the whole kingdom of Klue does."

"Especially us," Gabby said. "We'll take care of the frog for you."

"I know you do, girls." A tired smile stretched across Mr. Posh's face. "It's not your fault, don't worry. Now, how about another—"

But before he could say "curtsy," a shriek echoed through the palace.

Chapter Two

The Art of Invisibility

In one of the palace bathrooms, a woman knelt over the claw-footed bathtub. With a furious grunt, she banged the gold-plated faucet with a wrench.

"Miss Fix-It!" Mr. Posh said. "What in the world is the matter?"

Miss Fix-It was the palace handywoman. She could fix almost anything. She turned to face them with a wave of her wrench. "Every pipe in this bathroom is clogged! I have to get

them fixed before the Grand Ball tonight. And then these ... these frogs! They just showed up out of nowhere!"

Gabby crept silently across the bathroom floor, careful not to alert the invader frogs to her presence. A good ninja always practices the art of invisibility! This gives the ninja the advantage of surprise. The others watched her as she crept, crept, crept, then popped up to peer into the sink. Four plump green frogs peered back at her, their throats moving up and down silently.

Ava followed her sister's lead, creeping stealthily toward the shower. Creep, creep, creep, sweep! She swept the curtain aside and looked into the shower. Ten thin green frogs looked back. "Ribbit!" one croaked.

Ava relaxed her ninja stance. She closed the shower curtain and sighed. "Something is definitely fishy around here."

"Not fishy," Gabby laughed. "Froggy."

"I have to finish setting up the ballroom," Mr. Posh said. "Do you need help?"

Miss Fix-It turned back to the tub with a grunt. "I'll get it figured out."

"We can help you, Mr. Posh," Gabby said.

Mr. Posh pointed at Erk's head sticking out of Ava's pocket. "I don't want to see or hear any more frogs. Do you understand?"

"Yes, Mr. Posh," Ava and Gabby said in unison.

A few minutes later, they were in the Grand Ballroom. Tuxedoed workers scurried about, setting delicious desserts on six long tables. There were French apple tarts, red velvet cupcakes, and marshmallow butterscotch pie. And of course, Gabby's favorite: gooey triple chocolate brownie cookies.

They tried to blend into the scene to watch for anything suspicious. But the aromas were making it hard. Gabby wanted to taste every single thing.

"I'm so hungry," she whispered.

"You're always hungry," Ava whispered back.

"Ribbit," came a loud noise from nearby.

Several workers looked up, frowning. Across the room, Mr. Posh stood beside the table of honor. He narrowed his eyes at them.

"Shh, Erk! Mr. Posh will get mad if he knows we snuck you in here," Gabby whispered.

"Not me," Erk croaked in an offended tone.

"Erk is irked," Ava said, grinning. "Get it?"

"Ribbit," came again. "Ribbit, ribbit, ribbit."

Dozens of ribbits chorused around them.

The sounds were coming from everywhere!

Mr. Posh's face got red. Then it turned white. Ava and Gabby thought he might faint.

"Oh, no!" Gabby said.

Ava leaned down, grabbed the lace tablecloth, and lifted it up.

"Be careful!" Gabby steadied the crystal dishes before they fell over. "What do you see?"

"It's bananas!" Ava cried.

"Not bananas," Erk croaked. "Frogs!"

Gabby ducked down and looked too. At least twenty green frogs were huddled together beneath the table. They gazed up at Ava and Gabby with big, unblinking eyes. They flicked out their long, sticky tongues.

Gasps and shrieks filled the air as the waitstaff discovered more tiny green creatures

hidden beneath every single table. There were dozens of them. Maybe hundreds!

"Frogs!" Mr. Posh yelped. "The palace has been invaded by frogs!"

25

Chapter Three

Invasion!

"You know what this is," Gabby said in a quiet voice. "One frog is a surprise. Ten is a problem. A hundred is—"

"A mystery!" Ava sang excitedly. "Hooray! Time to put on our thinking crowns!"

With the golden crowns placed firmly on their heads, they were ready to crack the case.

"How did all these frogs get in here?" Ava asked. "Where did they come from? Did someone plant them here on purpose?"

"One question at a time." Gabby pulled out her pink, sparkly notebook and her fluffy unicorn pen. "Why would someone want to bring a bunch of frogs into the palace?"

Ava and Gabby looked at each other.

"To sabotage the Grand Ball," Ava replied. "But who would want to ruin such a splendid celebration?"

"We need to figure out the means, motive, and opportunity," Gabby said.

Ava pushed her glasses up the bridge of her nose. "Let's start with motive."

Gabby stared down at her notebook with a frown. She wrote **Suspects** at the top of a blank page. Then, under that, she scrawled in neat letters: **Mr. Posh**.

"Mr. Posh!" Ava cried. "But he's our friend!"

"Detectives treat everyone the same," Gabby reminded her. "We can't let our biases or feelings get in the way of solving the case."

"I know." Ava didn't want to suspect anyone they cared about, but Gabby was right. "Mr. Posh has to miss his own birthday to plan the Grand Ball. There are circles under his eyes *and* he lost his temper, which he never does."

Gabby nodded. "If the Grand Ball is canceled, he gets to enjoy his birthday and relax. He definitely has a motive."

"But what about means and opportunity? He's been working all day. How would he have time to sneak out and cart in a bunch of amphibians?"

"We haven't interviewed the rest of the palace," Gabby said. "Someone might have seen something we didn't."

"And how would Mr. Posh catch them all, anyway?" Ava asked. "Frogs are not easy to catch!"

"One thing at a time," Gabby said. "What do we always say? When in doubt—"

"Interview more witnesses!" Ava sang.

"Hop to it!' Erk croaked, making the princesses giggle.

"Everyone here is a potential witness," Gabby said.

"Or a potential suspect," Ava said. "It was an inside job. Someone who has access to our dressing room, the royal bathrooms, and the ballroom."

Maybe Mr. Posh really was guilty. But good detectives never jumped to conclusions. They needed to put in the legwork to solve this case!

For the next two hours, Ava and Gabby interviewed everyone they saw. The royal chefs didn't notice anything unusual. The housekeepers, busy dusting the silk tapestries and crystal chandeliers, didn't see anything suspicious either.

The princesses questioned the gardeners and the butler, the footmen, and even the grooms in the stables. No one knew anything. No one saw Mr. Posh or anyone else acting strangely.

Finally, Ava and Gabby tracked down Miss Fix-It again. She was pushing a cart of bird cages down the wide palace hall. Piles of frogs covered the floor of each cage.

"Did you catch all the frogs?" Ava asked hopefully.

"Heavens no," Miss Fix-It said unhappily. "There are hundreds of them! There's no way we can get rid of them before the Grand Ball. The queen will have to cancel it."

"We can't cancel!" Gabby cried. "The entire kingdom looks forward to it every year!"

"It's like Christmas in July!" Ava said. "Just without the presents."

Miss Fix-It shook her head glumly. "We don't have a choice."

"Have you seen any suspicious characters?" Gabby asked. "Anything out of the ordinary?"

"I spent my afternoon trying to fix the clogged pipes," Miss Fix-It said. "I didn't have time to notice anything else."

Ava pushed up her glasses. "Where are you taking them?"

Miss Fix-It pushed the cart past them. "Back to the pond, where frogs belong!"

Ava and Gabby watched her until she rounded the corner.

"She's right," Ava said. "They must have come from the pond."

Gabby nodded. "If we can figure out how the frogs got here, maybe we can solve the case and send them back the same way they came, saving the Grand Ball!"

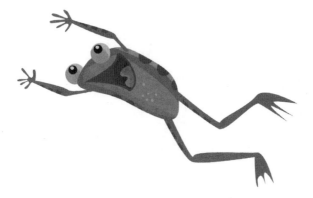

Chapter Four

No Can Do

O utside, the sun was shining. A pair of dragons swooped and circled the white, puffy clouds in the clear blue sky. The palace lawn was perfectly cut. Out past the moat that circled the palace, the water in the pond sparkled like diamonds.

There were no frogs to be seen anywhere.

The princesses weaved quickly around the footmen waiting for the Grand Ball

guests to arrive. Then they dashed across the drawbridge and darted down to the pond.

Careful not to dirty her dress, Gabby squatted at the water's edge. Her sparkly shoes sank into the mud. She pulled out her purple, jewel-covered magnifying glass.

The cattails were undisturbed. There were no human footprints. No frog prints, either.

Gabby stood up, took a step, and looked back. She'd left a perfect print of her shoe in the mud. "It rained last night. The ground is still wet. If someone came down here to catch all the frogs, there would be evidence."

"The fact that there are no clues is a clue in itself," Ava said.

"Right. No one took the frogs from the pond." Gabby touched her thinking crown. At the moment, it didn't seem to be helping. "Maybe Mr. Posh isn't guilty after all."

"We still don't know how the frogs got inside the castle or why." Ava looked down at the bump in the pocket of her dress. "Erk, you're a frog."

"That I am." Erk's voice was croakier than usual.

"Can you talk to the other frogs for us?"

"No can do," Erk said so softly they could barely hear him.

"Why not?"

Erk didn't say anything. But Ava's pocket trembled.

"Can you please come out and talk to us, Erk?" Gabby asked.

"He seems really scared," Ava said.

"Hmm," Gabby said.

Erk was scared of a lot of things. Heights. Water. The palace cat, Mouser, who was actually harmless. Even going outside gave Erk hives. He was a sensitive frog.

"Another dead end." Gabby stared at the pond in growing frustration. "Back to the drawing board."

"We're running out of time!" Ava pointed behind Gabby. "The first guests are arriving."

A white carriage rolled up to the castle entrance. Several more carriages waited in line behind it. "Race you back!" Gabby cried.

A footman helped the principal of Dragon Elementary School climb out. Principal Knight waved at Ava and Gabby as they ran up to her, panting from the sprint. She frowned down at Ava's hand, where Erk sagged, his tiny arms flung out dramatically. "Why does your frog look like he's dying?"

"Um, he doesn't like the heat," Gabby said with a shrug. "He's more of an indoor frog."

Principal Knight's eyebrows lifted to her hairline. "An indoor frog? I've never heard of such a thing."

"He's a frog prince," Ava explained.

"Maybe a human prince stuck as a frog," Gabby said.

"He might be waiting for one of us to kiss him."

Principal Knight pressed her lips together. "That's..."

Ava grinned. "Disgusting."

Gabby made a face. "Just ... ewww."

"So ... he'll be waiting for a while, then," Principal Knight said with a small smile.

"Exactly," said Gabby.

"Principal Knight," a footman said, "please wait here for a few moments. There's been a slight delay."

"Is everything okay?" Principal Knight asked.

Behind her, Miss Olsen, Mr. Harris, and Sensei Suki, all teachers at Dragon Elementary, climbed from a bright orange carriage. In the pink carriage next to them, Ava and Gabby's friends Mateo, Jade, and David leaned out of the windows, waving excitedly.

Everyone wore lovely gowns and handsome suits. They all looked so happy.

The footman frowned. "We'll let you know as soon as we can. For now, please remain here."

Ava grabbed Gabby's arm and pulled her away from the growing crowd of confused guests. "We have to do something!"

"We're out of time!" Gabby whispered.

"I have an idea," Ava said as they hurried back toward the castle. "I'll explain on the way!"

Chapter Five

Happy Birthday, Mr. Posh

Ava and Gabby burst through the ballroom doors. Mom and Dad were dressed in their royal finery. Mr. Posh, Miss Fix-It, and several other royal officials were defending the dessert tables from the green army. Frogs hopped across the shiny ballroom floor. They sat on the plush chairs. They plopped on the tables and tasted from the crystal glasses with their sticky tongues.

"I'm so sorry," Mom said sadly. "We must cancel the Grand Ball."

"Not yet!" Gabby pleaded. "We have a plan."

"Make it quick," Dad said as he brushed a frog away from a fancy bowl nearly overflowing with cotton candy-flavored punch.

"Where do the pipes in the royal bathrooms lead?" Gabby asked Miss Fix-It.

"Straight to the pond," Miss Fix-It replied.

Ava's hunch was correct. "No one brought the frogs here," she said. "That's why the pipes got clogged. The frogs came through the pipes on their own."

"But why?" Dad asked.

"Time to talk turkey, you frogs," Gabby said, looking around at the uninvited guests.

Ava rolled her eyes. "It's time to talk frog."

Erk gave a sad croak. He tried to hop off

Ava's hand. She closed her fingers, careful not to crush him. "Nice try. It's time to confess, Erk. The frogs are here for you, aren't they?"

Erk nodded his little green head.

Sometimes ninja princess detectives needed to be tough to get the truth. "Erk," Gabby said sternly.

Erk slumped in Ava's hand. "I'm a prince."

"We know that."

"A frog prince."

"We know that, too—"

"The humans speak Ribbit!" croaked an enormous green frog sitting on the table of honor. A tiny gold crown ringed his head. "I am Rib, King of the Frogs. And Erk is my son."

"You're not a prince trapped as a frog!" Ava sputtered to Erk. "You're a frog that's a prince!"

Erk looked up at Ava with one unblinking eye. "I told you."

He was right. They hadn't listened closely enough. Ava's cheeks turned bright red. For detectives, they'd sure missed a big clue.

"But if you're a frog prince, why do you stay with us?" Gabby asked.

"Because ... I like you," Erk croaked. "And I don't like water."

"The frog prince hates his pond home," the frog king bellowed. "He dislikes the outdoors!"

Erk lowered his head in shame. "Must I return?"

King Rib puffed out his chest. "I'll allow Erk to remain here. But I miss my son. If he won't come to us, then all of us will come to him. For short visits, of course."

Erk hopped happily toward his father.

"Thank you, Dad!"

"What are they saying?" Mom whispered.

Ava and Gabby grinned at each other. Though they could speak Ribbit, everyone else just heard loud croaking. Ava and Gabby quickly explained everything.

"Let's make a second table of honor for our fine frog friends," Dad boomed. "I'm sure our chefs can whip up some delicious, um, uh..."

"Fly soup, please," Erk croaked.

"The green guests would like fly soup," Ava said.

"Yuck," Gabby said.

Everyone laughed.

Mr. Posh hurried off toward the kitchen.

"Where are you going, Mr. Posh?" Mom said. Her warm smile widened. She patted the golden chair next to hers. "This seat of honor

52

is for you. Did you think we'd forget? Happy birthday!"

Mr. Posh's eyes glistened with happy tears.

Mom held out her palm to let the frog king hop into her hand. "What are we waiting for? Bring in the rest of the guests!"

"Time to dance!" Ava squealed as all the citizens of Klue poured through the ballroom doors.

Ava and Gabby greeted their guests with perfect curtsies as Mr. Posh watched proudly.

He didn't even mind that Ava had kicked off her shoes. Or that her shoes were full of frolicking frogs.

NPD Academy

Ninja Basics

In ancient Japan, ninjas were expert warriors and spies. They were trained in martial arts from a young age. They learned to fight, but they preferred to use stealth.

Ninjas wore dark clothes so they could hide in the dark. They wore special socks instead of shoes to sneak around quietly. They also had metal claws they put on their feet to climb the walls of tall buildings.

Some people thought ninjas had magical powers. They believed ninjas could fly and even walk on water. While they weren't magical, ninjas were strong, skilled, patient, and smart problem-solvers!

Super Ninja Skills You Can Use

Focus

An important thinking skill, focus helps a ninja—and you—put all your attention and effort into something to complete a task. Ninjas use their mental abilities to block out distractions as they work. Next time you're doing homework, pay attention to everything that distracts you. Then try shifting into ninja mode. Block out the distractions until your homework mission is complete!

Invisibility

Ninjas aren't actually invisible, but they can hide in plain sight! Ninjas are known for their ability to remain completely still and blend in with their environment. Try it at home, but be careful not to scare anyone!

Writing Mysteries

Mysteries are a genre, or category, of literature that focus on solving a mysterious problem, crime, or situation. A mystery has five basic elements:

1. **The mystery!** A pet goes missing. A favorite toy is stolen. Something strange happens, and no one knows why.

2. **The detective(s).** The detective is the character who investigates the situation, interviews witnesses, and eventually solves the case.

3. **Clues.** Clues are evidence that help lead the detective to the solution. And then there are red herrings! A red herring is a fake clue that authors put in a mystery to throw the detective (and the reader!) off the right track.

4. **The suspect(s).** Every good mystery has at least one suspect, or person the detective thinks is responsible. Two or three suspects makes it harder to solve the case. The detective must collect evidence to prove the suspect is guilty.

5. **The solution!** Solving the case is the best part of every mystery. The detective puts all the clues together and figures out the answer to the puzzle. The real clues need to make sense and help the detective crack the case.

Try It!
Ask a friend or family member to give you a person's name, an object, and a place. Now you have a character, a stolen object, and a setting! Write a mystery story based on these prompts.

Make a Frog Friend

Make a frog just like Erk!

Supplies

- white paper plate
- green washable paint
- paintbrush
- green, white, black, and red construction paper
- plastic cup (for tracing)
- pencil
- scissors
- glue
- black marker

Directions

1. Paint the back of the paper plate green.

2. While the paint is drying, turn over a plastic cup on the white construction paper. Use the pencil to trace the rim twice to draw two circles. Cut out each circle.

3. Cut two smaller circles and a crescent shape from the black construction paper.

4. Cut a strip from the red paper about one inch (2.54 centimeters) wide and three inches (7.62 centimeters) long.

5. Trace each of your hands on the green construction paper. Cut them out.

6. Glue the green hands to the underside edge of the paper plate to make the frog's feet.

7. Glue the two large white circles near the top of the plate side by side. Glue the smaller black circles inside the white circles to make the frog's eyes.

8. For the mouth, glue the black crescent to the center of the plate.

9. Wrap the red strip around a pencil to curl it. Glue it in the center of the mouth. Glue just enough to keep it attached while letting it curl up.

10. Do you speak Ribbit? Use the marker to write a word from that language along your frog friend's tongue!

About the Author

Kyla Steinkraus has been writing stories since she was five years old. Before she could write, she told stories into a recorder. Her parents still have some of them! Kyla lives with her two kids, her husband, and two very spoiled cats in Atlanta, Georgia. When she's not writing, Kyla loves hiking in the mountains, reading awesome books, and playing board games with her family. She has been known to jump out of a plane occasionally—parachute included, of course!

About the Illustrator

Katie Wood has loved drawing since she was very small, which inspired her to study illustration at Loughborough University. She now feels extremely lucky to be drawing every day from her studio in Leicester, England. She is never happier than when she is drawing with a cup of tea, or walking in the countryside with her unhelpful studio assistant, Inka the dog.